For A.B. and everyone else
who knows that this is a true story.

Where's Home?

By Gabrielle Israelievitch

Illustrations by Juliana Neufeld

TRIAD PUBLISHING CO. ● GAINESVILLE, FLORIDA

Library of Congress Cataloging-in-Publication Data

Israelievitch, Gabrielle, 1955-
     Where's home? / by Gabrielle Israelievitch ; illustrations by
Juliana Neufeld. -- 1st ed.
               p. cm.
     Summary: A young cat and his brothers and sisters are taken
away from their unfit parents and, after a time, find new families
that take better care of them.
     ISBN 978-0-937404-72-0
     [1. Cats--Fiction.   2. Foster home care--Fiction.]
I. Neufeld, Juliana, 1982- ill.   II. Title.   III. Title: Where is home?
PZ7.I86Wh 2011
[E]--dc22
                    2010030358

For informati;on regarding quantity orders,
contact Special Sales Dept., Triad Publishing Company,
P.O. Box 13355, Gainesville, FL 32605
or email orders@triadpublishing.com

www.triadpublishing.com

Contents

1

Littleprints Is Born

Once upon a place in a time far away a spunky black and green kitten was born to a Mr. and Mrs. Bob Cat, along with a litter of many, all on the same day, in just the way cats do.

Ma and Pa Bob had never had kittens before and they didn't know what to expect. Now, all at once, they had three yellow kittens and one odd fellow who was black and green, and different.

Confused, they looked at each other.

Ma asked, "How did this frog get here?"

As the three yellow kittens curled close to their Ma, the one who was different got up. He pushed himself up onto three of his four little legs, balancing there for a second before he collapsed. He raised himself again, this time on all fours.

Wobbling, he picked up his right forepaw and his left hindpaw. Then moved his left forepaw and right hindpaw and right forepaw and before he knew it, he'd propelled himself forward and just kept going like a wind-up toy.

He padded across the floor through a muddy puddle (right in the middle of the kitchen!) leaving one perfect paw print after another behind him.

By the time he stopped, muddy prints were everywhere, but his parents didn't mind in the least. They were happy that their little guy was so determined and they were happy that he was really a kitten after all.

He came back and snuggled against Ma in between the others. She rocked him and purred. Pa mewed in pride.

From that moment on, they called him Littleprints.

And Littleprints liked that.

2

Too Many Cats

Ma and Pa were in a great mood that day when Little-prints and his yellow sisters (Daisy, Daffodil and Sunshine) were born. But it didn't last.

After a very short while, along came another litter, then another. Pretty soon there were eight then twelve, and . . . well, too many kittens to count!

There was Bucky, who looked so much like Little-prints they were soon mistaken for twins (but at least not for frogs). With him came Tulip, Rosie and Poppy, then Spot, Harry and Tom. There were so many new ones they ran out of names. One thing was sure: This was a *WAY* bigger brood than Ma and Pa Bob could manage. They snarled and pounced, clawed and bit at each other for what seemed like no reason at all to Littleprints.

Every time Ma and Pa started to fight, all the kittens scurried for cover under the torn-up sofa. Huddled together and hearts racing, they cringed at the racket.

Once, when Littleprints dared to peek out, he saw blood! (You have to admit, seeing blood is pretty scary.)

The kittens never knew what to expect.

One morning when Ma and Pa were fighting again, Ma let out a piercing yowl. After some snarling and hissing from Pa, a door slammed.

In the silence that followed, the kittens cautiously crept out from under the sofa. One by one they climbed to the wide window sill. By the time the last one peered out, he only caught a glimpse of the black tip of Ma's tail as she dashed away from the house. Yes, she left, just like that, without a word—can you imagine?

Then, *thud!*

The kittens quickly turned toward the sound. Pa had collapsed into a furry heap on the filthy floor. A can of catnip was spilling out next to him.

They froze. They didn't know what would happen next. Would Pa wake up and go thrashing about like a monster? Would he wake up and go out after Ma? Or would he lie there and snore for a very long time?

The kittens watched. They waited. They worried.

Pa became a snoring machine. *What a relief!*

Now they were free to play, and off they went, scampering in all directions.

3

Between Snore and Slam

While Pa Bob snored like a lawnmower, the kittens climbed all over the furniture and tore at it with their sharp little claws till the stuffing came out. They leapt after the fluffy puffs and chased them around. They pounced on each other. They played and slept whenever and wherever they wanted.

When they were hungry, they ate any crumb or critter they could find. Sometimes they shared. Sometimes they fought. When one got hurt or felt bad, there was no one to offer comfort.

Anyway, you can see that there were good things and bad things about not having their parents around. But just as they got used to it . . .

Slam!

Ma was back. Seeing her kittens jumping all over the place, she snarled and hissed at them. She hissed as she locked them up in the cupboard with no food and no litterbox. She hissed at them when they whimpered and scratched their claws against the door.

The kittens were so scared that some of them pooped right there in the cupboard. It was too dark to know who had done what. Besides, they just wanted to get out, which didn't happen until Ma ran out of hissing that day.

There were also times, and you never knew when, Ma was suddenly playful. Like the day when she took all the kittens, even the teeny ones, for a climb and a tumble down the grassy hill. They climbed up and then they tumbled down until they were all on top of each other in one big laughing pile.

There in that heap, Ma gave Littleprints a special nuzzle and rocked him for a few moments for what seemed like no reason at all to Littleprints. It did feel especially nice, though.

4

Dream Floes

Often Littleprints did not have a nice feeling inside. Sometimes he curled up into a ball and rocked back and forth. He felt a little better doing that. He rocked and rocked until he fell asleep. And when he slept, he dreamed…

Carry me crystal there
huge white bear
onto ice
and cool
in a pool of light
where we share a bite, and sleep
sleep and swim
hide and seek and
rock at sea.
Twinkle, twinkle little glass stars.

When Littleprints awoke his dreams broke apart and floated away.

5

The Marble

Ma and Pa Bob weren't the kinds of cats who gave their kittens toys, but over time, on this outing or that, each of the kittens discovered some little treasure to play with.

One sunny morning, Littleprints noticed a small crystal ball twinkling on the edge of the gutter. He approached it with curiosity (he was a cat, after all) and saw to his great delight that it was a marble!

Ever so carefully, so it wouldn't roll down the drain, Littleprints swatted the sparkling marble away from the gutter and onto the dusty road and down the grassy hill. He rolled his new marble all the way home. For a while, he rolled it everywhere . . . until it was lost.

Rosie's treasure was a bright red rubber band. She zigzagged and zipped about, snapping and chasing it. Seeming to dance in mysterious spurts, she looked like a sprite.

Spot collected odd bits of cardboard. Clearly an artist,

he scratched pictures in them with his claws, often trying to draw his brothers and sisters.

One afternoon, Bucky discovered a long, orange string that was attached to an empty box. He tugged and tugged and finally managed to get it free. Proudly, he thrashed his new string about as if it were a live snake. When he got tired, he dragged it the rest of the way home.

The kittens always had someone to play with. They posed for Spot's pictures, played tug-of-war with Bucky, snapped and chased Rosie's rubber band, and hunted for Littleprints' lost marble.

One day, when there had been a new batch of baby kittens in the corner for a week or so, one of them began making an awful sound.

What was that sound?

Ma was nowhere to be seen. Littleprints scampered over to the new, not-yet-named kitten and saw that she was choking!

He pounded her on the back (gently, for she was such a tiny thing) and you'll never believe this: Littleprints' marble rolled out of her mouth!

Littleprints was happy twice. The new little kitten

didn't choke *AND* he'd found his marble. It was then that Littleprints saw for the first tme that this was a cat's-eye marble, a small, clear globe with an inner eye of green and black. When he looked at it, it was as though his own eye looked back at him.

Littleprints glanced around for Ma, but she was still nowhere to be seen. He nuzzled the tiny kitten so she wouldn't be scared (and also to thank her). When he felt she was calm, he got up and searched for a safe place to stash his marvelous marble.

After some scouting, Littleprints discovered a pouch in the rip of the sofa where he could place his marble safely. He was pleased. And for a while it just stayed there.

6

The Wink

For Littleprints and his brothers and sisters, time continued to be marked by random snores and slamming doors. Sometimes life was terrible and sometimes it was not so bad. Besides, it was the only life they knew. So when they weren't busy worrying (or napping or fighting), they did what kittens love best of all: they played.

Once in a while, when he was alone, Littleprints was able to pull out his green cat's-eye marble. In a certain light it looked like a twinkling star. Sometimes it seemed to wink at him. He began to wonder at its marvels. He didn't tell Bucky or anyone. He tucked it away again in the sofa.

When it was too crowded or too dark to play with his marble, Littleprints sometimes washed little Poppy or Spot or Rosie with his tongue, just as he saw Daffodil washing Harry or the others. Sometimes he nuzzled the sweet, new little kitten.

Since no one had named her, he called her "Marble."

And Marble liked that.

In general, though, it didn't occur to anyone to clean up the place or take care of each other. So they were mostly dirty and hungry and didn't know how to act so they could feel safe.

Oh, and they were loud.

7

About the Mice

Living alongside the Bob Cat family, in spaces small enough that cats couldn't reach, were Ma and Pa Nice Mice with their own lively brood.

The Nice Mice family was even larger than the Bob Cats', but their aunts and uncles and cousins and grandmas and grandpas all worked together to keep their home tidy and to keep their children fed and clean and safe. Rarely did things get out of hand.

One day, the mice children were doing their home-work in "How to Avoid Cats and Mousetraps," and the kittens were making a lot of noise. On their side of the wall, Marvin, the oldest and most outspoken of the young mice, stomped his paw.

"I, for one, have had enough! I don't care if I'm supposed to avoid cats, I am going to take myself Over There and tell them to *BE QUIET!* There certainly isn't anyone else to tell them."

"And how would you know that?" asked Ma Nice.

She looked him sternly in the eye. "Have you been Over There, Marvin?"

"Uhh . . . nnnot exactly," replied Marvin. "It's just that those guys make so much noise that sometimes I creep up to the wall and wriggle into a little crack to see what is going on. I was just looking. Honest."

"Me, too," peeped Micro.

"Me, too," squeaked Moto, and suddenly the place was all a-twitter with this group confession.

"Were you wearing your helmets?" Ma asked.

"Of course, Ma," they answered together.

She sighed. "I've also been very curious. I'm glad to know you were careful. We'll talk about this later."

And like most mothers who say that, she forgot.

"For now, let's hear what you've seen."

8

What the Mice Saw

Marvin spoke first. "I've seen the kittens tearing up the furniture and playing in the mess. Once a wee little kitten cut himself on a piece of glass from the broken window and he licked his own paw!"

He paused to see that everyone was listening, and continued, "Once, Mr. Cat was opening the big white fridge and I saw rows and rows of catnip and nothing else in there."

"I saw a kitty gagging . . ." said Micro.

"Yeah, I saw that! And another kitten knocked a crystal ball out of her mouth!" exclaimed Mini.

Moto added, "I saw lots of kittens all dirty with their fur stuck to them. And I saw Mrs. Cat locking them up in a closet!"

Many had seen litter boxes upside down and smeared and scattered about. All the mice were soon muttering at once about these strange cat customs.

Ma Nice said, "Now that I've heard all your stories, I am wondering if there's something very wrong in the Bob

Cat family. Marvin, I think you had the right idea when you said there was no one in charge Over There. Who is taking care of all those kittens?"

At dinner that night the whole Nice Mice family— the young ones and their parents and aunts and uncles and cousins and grandmas and grandpas—began wondering together about the lives of these kittens with whom they shared a wall.

"What about the noise?" asked Marvin. "I say we go shout at them."

"How will that help the kittens?" peeped little Moto.

"Help kittens?" cried Marvin. "We're talking about CATS here."

"Enemies!"

"Maybe we can help and still stay safe," suggested Ma.

"What can we do?" they all chimed.

They had not yet heard from Grandma Nice. They turned to her as she said, "There is one thing we can do that will keep us safe and protect the kittens. We can write a note to the Humane Society."

And so they did. They wrote:

Dear Humane Society,

We Have seen very SAD things at 321 Cat Alley, the home of Mr. and Mrs. Robert (BOB) cat and their many, many kittens. At least, these things are SAD to us mice. Perhaps they are cat customs, but please do go take a look and see if you think those kittens are safe.

Yours Sincerely,
The Nice Mice Family

9

The Day the Bears Came

On the day the Humane Society received the Mice family letter, they instantly dispatched their team of Bears to check on the little Bob Cats and get them to safety if necessary.

Before long, a large Bear stood checking his clipboard at the door of 321 Cat Alley, home of the Bob Cat family. He was wearing a blue bow tie and had a brown canvas satchel slung over his shoulder. His team hung back in the shade.

The Bear knocked. No one answered. He checked his clipboard again, then he pounded, shouting, "Open up!"

Pa Bob appeared warily with Ma close behind him. "Yeah?" they snarled through the half-opened door. An awful smell came from inside the house.

The Bear cleared his throat. "Sir. Madam. My name is Mr. Ted E. Bear, B-E-A-R, and I have been sent by the Humane Society. We have had a report that your kittens

28

are not being properly cared for. We need to come in and have a look around."

He gave a signal for his team to join him.

Pa hollered, "You have no right" but Mr. Ted E. Bear held up his clipboard and said, "I do. Please let us in."

Thereupon the Bear Team entered the Cats' home. They looked around. A stunned and stern Bear declared to Mr. and Mrs. Bob Cat, "There is broken glass everywhere. The springs poke out of the sofa where the kittens play and sleep. The place smells like catnip and poop. Your kittens are dirty and hungry. This is not a safe place for them. By law, I must take them away."

Ma and Pa Bob now stood silently, but the kittens, who'd hidden all together under the sofa, howled, "We don't want to leave Ma and Pa. We're fine."

But no one seemed to pay any attention.

At the Bears' coaxing, the kittens came slowly from under the arms and the front and the back and through the seat of the sofa. Some of the kittens wept. They had all clearly understood the words "take them away."

Mr. Ted E. Bear scrunched himself small and spoke quietly to the kittens so as not to frighten them further. He said, "I know it is hard to leave your Ma and Pa, but we are here to help you and to keep you safe."

Before any of them could make sense of what was happening, the kittens were divided up and sent with different Bears to different homes with different caregivers. Not one of them knew any word for how horrible this felt.

10

The Longest Day in the World

As the rest of the kittens were taken away in all directions, Mr. Ted stayed with Littleprints and Bucky. He said, "Before we leave, why don't you go collect something that you'd like to keep with you."

Littleprints, of course, went to the pouch in the rip of the sofa. But instead of pulling his marble out, he climbed inside and curled himself around it. He was remembering that he'd hidden it here to protect his tiny sister.

Where had she gone? When would he see her again?

He slipped into his dream where he swam and played with the polar bears.

Once Bucky found his orange string, Mr. Ted scooped up Littleprints, still sleeping and curled around his marble. They made their way outside, and when Littleprints awoke, Mr. Ted placed him on the ground under the shady trees.

He removed his bow tie and stuffed it into his satchel with the clipboard. Then, for what seemed like no reason at

all, Bucky suddenly zipped away. He started zigging and zagging and whipping his string at the air. He was out of control.

Mr. Ted fetched Bucky, saying to him in a loud but kind voice, "This feels no fair! How could someone break apart your family? It is so scary, having to go live with cats you don't know."

When he felt Bucky's wildness calm, Mr. Ted pulled two green velvet boxes from his satchel. They had furry backstraps to make them comfy to wear.

He said, "I have a special box for each of you. It's for your treasures. Inside you'll also find a key."

"A key to what?" asked Bucky.

"A key to any Box Club—that's a place where there are special cats who play games and talk with you. Your sisters and brothers will get green boxes and keys, too. You might be able to see them sometime when you're there."

Bucky looked down and swirled his string in the dirt, knocking the bow tie from the open satchel.

"Hey, Bear, your tie's on the ground." He whipped at it with his string. He snarled to himself.

Mr. Ted said, "Thank you, Bucky, for letting me know where my tie is," and he proceeded to help Littleprints open his box and put his marble inside. "May your treasures protect you and keep you safe."

"Whatever," said Bucky as he swished his orange string around the blue bow tie on the ground.

Rays of sun poked through the shimmery leaves. Littleprints glanced at his crystal green cat's-eye marble. At just that moment, his marble winked!

Right there. Right then.

Mr. Ted must have seen it, too, because he looked straight at Littleprints, smiled, and winked at him.

A wave of warmth filled up the inside of Littleprints. He didn't have a name for the way this felt. But he liked it.

They sat quietly for a few minutes, then Mr. Ted retrieved his bow tie and dusted it off.

"Littleprints, it's time now to close your box." He stood up, Littleprints stood up, and they went over to Bucky. It was time to go to their new home.

They began the long walk into the big forest to an unfamiliar place.

11

Strange New Faces

It was getting dark by the time they arrived at their new home. There seemed to be shadows everywhere.

Mr. Ted knocked.

"Auntie Cal," as she called herself, threw open the door and welcomed them in. Auntie Cal was an odd-looking cat. She looked an awful lot like a wolf dressed up as a cat. The Bob kittens took an instant dislike to her.

They looked around. They saw lots of other kittens. They saw a pile of green boxes like the ones Mr. Ted had given them. They saw a bowl of milk, several litter boxes, and a few ratty balls of string. It smelled strange.

"Don't leave us here," they pleaded to Mr. Ted.

They stood in the doorway with their boxes strapped to their backs and would not move.

Auntie Cal insisted, "Come in, boys. Take off your boxes and put them in the family pile."

They refused.

"These cats are not our family," they said.

Auntie Cal looked at Mr. Ted, who said. "Let them keep their stuff with them. They need to have something that's their own."

"Well, okay," she said, "but come on in, at least."

Once inside, the kittens noticed some cushions that looked like they'd once been a bright yellow, but were now worn and faded.

Mr. Ted said, "I have to leave, but I'll be back for a visit in three days."

"Don't go!" they protested.

Holding up two paws, Mr. Ted said, "Okay, I'll see you guys in *TWO* days," and with that, he left.

Littleprints went straight to a box to curl up inside. Bucky went straight to take a bite out of one of the younger kittens.

When Mr. Ted returned in two days, Auntie Cal sent Littleprints and Bucky with him because, she said, she wasn't able to keep everybody safe. Again, the kittens did not know what to expect. They continued to be moved from place to place.

Mr. Ted took them to Miss Ginger's house next, but all she wanted to do was nuzzle them. While that can be a nice idea if you know the nuzzler, Littleprints and Bucky did not know Miss Ginger. They wanted their Ma Bob. They remembered how nice it felt when she nuzzled them.

Bucky tied up Miss Ginger with his long, orange string. (Littleprints helped him a teeny little bit.) The next morning, Mr. Ted came back for the brothers.

12

The Club

Every Thursday, no matter what, no matter where they were, Mr. Ted came to get Littleprints and Bucky and take them to the Box Club. He had his own key, but he let the kittens take turns using theirs.

The first time they entered the Club, they saw it was clean and bright. There were lots of toys, things to climb, things to tear at, things to chase. Dr. Lynx and Ms. Jag, the special cats who were always around, spent time with them, one-to-one. Scrambling into this box or that, they built forts, played games, and told stories.

After a while, Littleprints showed Dr. Lynx his marble and they spent lots of time together playing with it. Sometimes it caught the light just right and sparkled. He thought of how he first saw that sparkle near a gutter, when he was on an outing with his real family.

He missed them. He thought that if he behaved very, very well he could go back to them. He didn't tell this to

Dr. Lynx, but somehow she understood.

Like Mr. Ted, Dr. Lynx had seen the Wink and she, too, had looked straightaway at Littleprints, smiled, and winked at him.

A number of times, Ma and Pa Bob called to talk to Littleprints and Bucky. They asked the boys what toys they wanted. They made plans to visit. Littleprints and Bucky got all excited and waited and waited for them to come. More often than not, they didn't.

Then they stopped calling.

These disappointments were more than the kittens could bear. You could even say they were heartbroken. Again and again.

Each kitten had his own way of showing his broken

heart. Bucky snarled and clawed at others, or he ran and climbed very high, farther and farther away from everyone.

Littleprints curled up in the smallest place he could find. He slept and dreamed, lulled by the twinkling of little glass stars.

As the weeks went on, the chance of getting back with their original family got smaller and smaller. The kittens still did not know what to expect. They did not know what to get used to.

13

Then One Day

Returning from an outing with a group of kittens and Auntie and Uncle Whoever-It-Was-This-Time, Littleprints and Bucky found Mr. Ted at their doorstep.

He said, "I have good news. I have found you a new home with cats who have lots of time and lots of care just for you."

Leaving Auntie and Uncle Whoever and their brood of assorted kittens was no big deal to Littleprints and Bucky, but they still were a bit nervous about moving to another new place.

That very day, Mr. Ted brought them to the other side of the forest to the very tidy home of Mr. and Mrs. Cool Cat. The windows sparkled in the sunlight.

Mr. Ted knocked.

Still wearing her apron, Mrs. Cool opened the door and a cheerful Mr. Cool was right by her side. The place was fragrant with freshly baking sweetfish pie.

"Welcome," they said together.

Littleprints clung his sharp claws into Mr. Ted's furry ankle as Mrs. Cool closed the door. She then scrunched herself small and looked at Littleprints. "I'm glad to meet you," she purred.

She stayed with him just like that, quiet and small.

Littleprints noticed that the place was bright and clean and warm. He let go of Mr. Ted's ankle. He slipped the green box from his back and put it on the floor.

Meanwhile, Bucky leapt wildly about with his orange string, screeching to a halt just before crashing into a bowl of milk.

"You must be Bucky," said Mr. Cool. "You are one busy cowboy!"

The Cools showed Mr. Ted, Bucky, and Littleprints around. They told the kittens where they could put their stuff, and they told them the rules of the house.

Ma and Pa Cool (as the kittens came to call them) showed them their very own corner with their very own cushions to sleep on. Pa Cool had placed a soft green blanket on Littleprints' silky cushion and a soft orange blanket on Bucky's. Each kitten had a little space and a little blanket of his own.

Ma Cool showed them the bowl of milk they would all share. She showed them the litterbox.

The adults let the kittens wander and peek, sniff, stretch, and settle as they chatted among themselves. When they finished their chatting, Mr. Ted said he was leaving but promised Littleprints and Bucky he would take them to the Club next Thursday. The kittens let him go without much fuss. They knew they would see him on Thursday.

The new foursome ate dinner together. Ma and Pa Cool asked the kittens questions . . . about school and about friends. But Littleprints and Bucky did not say much this very first evening. In a warm silence, they ate the sweetfish pie, every now and then mentioning how very delicious it was.

14

The Cool Cats

Littleprints and Bucky discovered that Ma Cool was usually busy during the day, chasing mice and all that, sometimes traveling quite far and getting home late. But Pa Cool was around all the time.

He walked with Littleprints and Bucky everywhere they needed to go—to have their nails clipped, to get their needles and shots, to have some lessons in rules and manners and life. Littleprints especially liked rules and manners because they helped him know what to expect.

By now, the kittens really knew they could have as much food as they were hungry for. But, as they'd done everywhere they'd lived, they continued sneaking off to their cushions with any extra food, just in case.

Ma and Pa Cool helped Littleprints clean the food off his velvet box, which he also kept under his cushion. They sat with the kittens when they did their homework. They fetched Bucky when he ran away. They purred quietly into Littleprints' ear when he rocked back and forth. They rubbed his sore shoulder when Bucky scratched him for what seemed to Littleprints like no reason at all. The four of them ate together and played together and calmed down together.

Every evening, Ma and Pa Cool nuzzled the kittens as they fell asleep on their soft, silky cushions and wrapped each of them in his own special blanket.

To the hushed purrs of lullabies, Littleprints and Bucky went to sleep every night in this clean place that smelled nice, always having had plenty to eat.

This is how they became a family.

15

Surprise!

On Thursday as promised, Mr. Ted picked up Little-prints and Bucky and took them to the Club. This Thursday it was Littleprints' turn to use his key. He opened the door, and who should be standing there in the lobby but his baby sister, little Marble!

She smiled. "Nice green pack. I have one just like it." Bucky pushed past them and went off with Ms. Jag.

Mr. Ted said to Marble, "Hmm. Didn't he recognize you? Anyway, why don't you and Littleprints go catch up with each other."

They readily agreed and Mr. Ted went off to the lounge to chat with the other adults.

Littleprints and Marble climbed together into an open box and stared at each other for a few moments.

Then Littleprints said, "We haven't seen each other since the Bears came."

"What an awful day that was! I was so nervous and upset. I felt so lost."

"Me, too.

"Where did they take you?"

"Actually, to a very nice home with the Tabby family. I was pretty little but one thing I remember at the beginning was *MEALS*. We had never heard of such customs! And now it seems normal for a family to be all together to eat and talk—and at the same time every day!

"Yeah," chimed in Littleprints. "And *BEDTIMES!* Is it the same for you?"

"Yes, and *SLEEPING CUSHIONS!*"

"Things are pretty good now," said Littleprints. "At first, I was moved around quite a bit. It wasn't so easy. Where I am now is good. I think it's Home."

"I'm glad for you, Littleprints. I feel like I belong where I am, too, but I've missed you."

She paused. "Have you seen anything of Ma or Pa Bob?"

"Not in ages. I don't even remember what they smell like."

"Same here. Makes me sad."

"Me, too. But now I see how nobody took care of us then."

"Well, *you* took care of me."

"I was not your parent, my little sister, but I felt a special bond with you when you rescued my marble, which by the way, I always keep with me."

"You rescued *me*, Littleprints. You gave me my life *and* my name. I always keep both with me, of course." She smiled. Then she said, "What's with Bucky?"

"You mean how he ignored you?"

"Yeah. That was awkward. I was glad to see him and then . . . nothing."

"I know what you mean about Bucky; I live with him. He mostly has one way of being, and that's in his own private angry world, especially if things don't go the way he wants."

"Why would he be mad at me?" asked Marble.

"He's just too angry to be interested in much besides being angry."

Mr. Ted peeked his head in and said it was time to go.

"Not already!" they said.

As they reluctantly crawled out of the box and walked back to the lobby, they exchanged addresses.

Bucky and Ms. Jag came to where the others were gathered. Bucky looked at Marble.

He said, "Hey."

"Hey," she replied, then continued to the door to wait for Ma Tabby. As Mr. Ted left with the Cool kittens for home, she said, "See ya."

"See ya, Marble."

Everybody waved goodbye. Littleprints grinned and frolicked all the way back. Bucky dragged his string.

That evening, Pa Cool took the boys out to the park. Their buddies were already scampering around in the twilight. Once the friends were all assembled, they climbed one by one up the slide. They piled on top of each other, paused, and pushed off, swooshing down together, squealing. They landed in a laughing heap at the bottom. Like the afternoons on the grassy hill with Ma Bob.

16

Little Prince

Littleprints was sometimes so good at rules and manners — like keeping his cushion tidy, like letting Ma take the first run at a house-mouse — that Pa Cool began calling him Little Prince. "Little Prince, Littleprints," he sang to himself.

One morning, the two of them were sitting together by Littleprints' silky cushion. They had just opened his green velvet box. Pa Cool stroked his son's head and admired his marble.

He said, "You know, Littleprints, I'm so proud of you. I'm so proud of all of us and how we are becoming a family. You are my real Little Prince.

"And you are My Most Real Highness, Old King Cool," replied Littleprints.

"And you are such a prince of a guy," added Pa with a twinkle in his eye.

The two of them were so much in the same dance of

play, they happened to look at the crystal green cats'-eye marble at just the same time.

Littleprints caught its wink. Pa Cool must have, too, for he looked straight at Littleprints, smiled, and winked. Sunshine filled up the inside of Littleprints.

17

The Fight

One day Bucky-the-Cowboy tied up Ma and Pa Cool with his orange string. It wasn't so hard for them to untie themselves from the string. Bucky was just a kitten, after all. But it was hard for them to undo the tangle of confusion they felt about how to be his parents. He had gone off in a huff. Out the door, without a word.

Littleprints wasn't paying attention. He was busy playing with a rubber band. Suddenly, there was a racket coming from across the room. He felt a familiar fear.

His heart racing, Littleprints scurried under the sofa. He held his breath. He waited. Was that Ma and Pa Cool? Were they fighting?

He began to shake and could not stop. For the first time in a very long time, he didn't know what to expect.

When Littleprints peeked out, his parents were meowing quite loudly at each other and sometimes at the same time. They were not snarling or hissing. They were not scratching at each other. There was no blood.

They were arguing, but not hurting each other. Littleprints watched and listened.

Pa Cool was saying, "There are special places for young cats who keep getting into fights or who run away when they still need care."

Ma Cool wept, saying, "He's so angry at the world. We just have to love him more."

"But how?" asked Pa.

"I don't know," answered Ma.

Now Littleprints understood. They were talking about Bucky.

Ma Cool wept some more, but Littleprints could see that Pa Cool had not hurt her. He could see from her tears and hear in her voice that Ma was sad. She was very sad because all her love and care were not helping Bucky feel better. They were yelling but they didn't seem angry at each other; they were just angry at the same time, and confused about Bucky.

"Let's call Mr. Ted," they said.

From under the sofa, Littleprints saw them nuzzle each other. But he was still shaking. He didn't know why. He was very sad, too. And he didn't know why.

Pa Cool said to Ma, "I'm going out to find Bucky."

Ma Cool said, "And I'm going to find Littleprints."

When she discovered him under the sofa, she scrunched herself small and asked, "Can I join you?"

"Yeah," he said.

She crawled under and settled next to him. She said, "That was pretty scary for you."

"Yeah," he said.

"You probably thought we were hurting each other."

"Yeah," said Littleprints and he snuggled into her. They stayed that way for a long time.

Even after he and Ma crawled out together from under the sofa, Littleprints was quiet for the rest of the evening.

18

Littleprints Reviews Things

Littleprints went to his cushion and got out his green velvet box from underneath. He placed it on top of the cushion. He opened his box, taking out one by one all the treasures he'd been secretly collecting.

He took out his baby teeth and the tooth fairy's first note to him that said, "Keep your special memories in your special box."

He took out the prints of his four little baby paws that he had made in one of his classes long ago. He laid out everything: his crystal green cat's-eye marble, the letters from his sister Marble, a tiny book with a note from Mr. Ted, the red rubber band that reminded him of Rosie, a thin thread of orange string he'd saved from the last time Bucky had tied him up. He even had a small piece of cardboard that made him think of Spot.

He surrounded his cushion with these things, each

one a part of the story of himself. He climbed on his cush-ion and curled up to sleep.

Later, after he found Bucky, Pa Cool came in and covered him.

19

Speak, Dreams

On a day that looked the same as all the others, Bucky ran away again. Far away this time. Ma and Pa Cool, the neighbors and the Bears all looked for him.

It was growing dark when Mr. Ted spotted him high in a tall tree on the other side of the hill. Bucky showed his teeth, clawed at the air, and roared like a lion. The Bears got him down.

Everyone knew what was next. Bucky had to go to a place where he and those around him would be safe.

Mr. Ted said, "While Bucky is at the safe place he will see a lot of Ms. Jag, who will be trying to understand what is best for him. I don't know if Bucky will come back here. Maybe it will be best for him if he gets to live with a family where he is the only kitten."

Ma and Pa Cool said nothing. It was Littleprints who spoke. "No matter what happens," he said, "I want us to visit Bucky, wherever he is. We have to be able to count on seeing him; he can't just disappear."

Ma and Pa, Mr. Ted, Littleprints and Bucky all agreed to set up regular visits.

Then they said goodbye, which was quite upsetting for everyone, though Bucky acted like he didn't care, which was upsetting in another way.

* * *

After a while, Littleprints began missing his brother. A lot. He felt horrible inside.

He went to Pa Cool, curled into him, and wept into his furry neck. Through his sobs he said, "Pa, I'm so sad that Bucky is gone. I'm lonely. There's no one for me to play with. No one to talk to at night. No one else who has had a whole life together with me. I miss him."

He sniffled and sat up, looking at Pa.

"But do you know what? I am also glad he's gone. He isn't here to scratch at me for no reason at all. He isn't here to be afraid of." Pa nodded. "And I get angry at him for being so hard to get along with. And then I feel sorry for him." He lay down again and curled into Pa.

"How can I feel all these things at once?"

Exhausted, he fell instantly into a dream and didn't hear one word of Pa's wise response.

* * *

On Thursday, Littleprints talked to Dr. Lynx about his special dream. "In my dream I feel cold and warm at the same time. I'm a small cat in the frozen Arctic. But with the bears I feel warm somehow. They stay close to me. They feed me. We swim and play."

Dr. Lynx said, "In your happy polar dreams you are part of a family . . ."

"Part of a family of *BEARS*. Bears, like Mr. Ted! "

Littleprints rolled his crystal green cat's-eye marble around as he spoke, watching it catch the light.

"This marble sparkles like the ice crystals in my dream," he said.

"Like you have a piece of your dream right here," said Dr. Lynx.

Littleprints looked up at her, "I have a funny thought. 'Cool' would be a good name for a polar bear family, but it's my cat family's name. Ma and Pa Cool aren't huge white bears, but they are pretty cool cats."

"They are cool cats, Littleprints," said Dr. Lynx. "And so are you."

20

And There You May Be

It is nighttime. Littleprints lies awake. He thinks about Marble and what she wrote to him last week. She told him that she had located the Nice Mice family and written to them! She is friends with Mice, if you can believe that!

Littleprints lies there in the dark, eyes wide open.

He thinks backward . . . back to the times with his brother, whooshing down the slide in the park, playing tug of war.

He thinks about Ma and Pa Bob and how he can't remember what they smell like.

He wonders whatever happened to the many, many brothers and sisters from his earliest life.

But Littleprints notices that for the first time he is thinking forward as well.

He is thinking about going to school every day where he'll see his friends.

He is thinking about having dinner together every

evening and being sung to every night by his parents.

He is thinking about visiting Bucky and getting letters from Marble.

He is thinking about how one day he might become an Arctic explorer, or an astronaut. And as he's thinking these things, the inside of him fills with sunshine.

* * *

Littleprints, or LP, as he's now called, can be found every Thursday at the Club on Gryphon Street, and if you get to know him in that place and time, or another, near or far, you may be with him just when his marble winks. And you'll know what to do.

For discussions about the story,
visit www.whereshome.me